Hello, yc

Oh, please don't look

inside the pages

of this **book**.

Turn around and quickly run ...

The SCHOOL of MONSTERS has begun!

THIS BOOK BELONGS TO

SCHOOL OF MONSTERS

By Sally Rippin

BUG'S FIRST DAY

Art by Chris Kennett

Kane Miller
A DIVISION OF EDC PUBLISHING

Monsters sit down on the **mat**.

They listen to their teacher, Pat.

They all sit close,
except for **Bug**.

He hides himself
under a **rug**.

ZOOP!

Monsters take a pad and **pen**.

6

They practice writing up to **ten**.

But Bug just throws
his on the **mat**,

then runs and hides
under a **hat**.

SWOOSH!

At last, their teacher rings the **bell**.

She asks poor Bug,
"Are you not **well**?"

Bug starts to cry.
His cheeks are **wet**.

"I don't know all my numbers **yet**!

"I can't read books or write my **name**.

To me, the words all look the **same**.

"I don't think school
is right for **me**.

GRAB

I can't do anything,
you **see**!"

PLOP

Teacher smiles.
She gives a **tug**

to little Bug,
who needs a **hug**.

"Oh Bug!" she says.
"Now, don't you **fret**.

No one here is perfect yet!"

"No way?" says Bug.
"It's not just **me**?"

"Of course," laughs Pat. "Just come and **see** ...

"I'm here to help you *learn* to **read**,

and any other
help you **need**.

"New things take time to learn to **do**."

"And guess what, Bug?

"We're learning **too!**"

"So now it's time to have some **fun**.

Go make some friends, run in the sun.

"You're here to learn, but also **play**.

There's *lots* of time.
It's your first **day**!"

NEW WORDS TO LEARN
me
pen
mat
well
Can you find all the words with double letters?
START HERE
NEXT LEVEL
WELL DONE
tug
too

do

ten

name

wet

Pat

day

hat

same

sun

fun

see

rug

play

read

need

Bug

bell

yet

fret

hug

HOW TO USE THIS BOOK

for adults reading with children

Welcome to the School of Monsters!

Here are some tips for helping your child learn to read.

At first, your child will be happy just to listen to you read aloud. Reading to your child is a great way for them to associate books with enjoyment and love, as well as to become familiar with language. Talk to them about what is going on in the pictures and ask them questions about what they see. As you read aloud, follow the words with your finger from left to right.

Once your child has started to receive some basic reading instruction, you might like to point out the words in **bold**. Some of these will already be familiar from school. You can assist your child to decode the ones they don't know by sounding out the letters.

As your child's confidence increases, you might like to pause at each word in bold and let your child try to sound it out for themselves. They can then practice the words again using the list at the back of the book.

After some time, your child may feel ready to tackle the whole story themselves. Maybe they can make up their own monster stories, too!

Sally Rippin is one of Australia's best-selling and most-beloved children's authors. She has written over 50 books for children and young adults, and her mantel holds numerous awards for her writing. Best known for her *Billie B. Brown*, *Hey Jack!* and *Polly and Buster* series, Sally loves to write stories with heart, as well as characters that resonate with children, parents, and teachers alike.

HOW TO DRAW

BUG

1 Using a pencil, start with 2 ovals for eyes. Add a happy little mouth and connect the eyes in the middle to turn them into glasses.

2 Now draw a big U shape for his tummy and a curved line for his head. Add 2 horns and a curved W shape for teeth.

3 Draw 2 boxes for his shorts and add 2 mountain shapes for the top of his wings.

4 Now draw 2 bird shapes for the bottom of the wings. Then add some tubes for his arms and legs.

5 Draw in his hands, some flipper frog feet, and 2 stripes for his belt. Use an eraser to remove the connecting lines, if you have one.

6 Time for the final details! Draw in some lines for eyebrows, for his belt buckle, and on his horns. Don't forget the spots on his belly!

Chris Kennett has been drawing ever since he could hold a pencil (or so his mom says). But professionally, Chris has been creating quirky characters for just over 20 years. He's best known for drawing weird and wonderful creatures from the *Star Wars* universe, but he also loves drawing cute and cuddly monsters – and he hopes you do too!

WELCOME
TO THE

SCHOOL OF MONSTERS

You shouldn't bring a pet to **school**. But Mary's pet is super **cool**!

SCHOOL OF MONSTERS
By Sally Rippin
MARY HAS THE BEST PET
Art by Chris Kennett

Have you read **ALL** the School of Monsters stories?

Sam makes a mess when he eats **jam**. Can he fix it? Yes, he **can**!

SCHOOL OF MONSTERS
By Sally Rippin
HAIRY SAM LOVES BREAD AND JAM

SCHOOL OF MONSTERS
By Sally Rippin
PETE'S BIG FEET
Art by Chris Kennett

Today it's Sports Day in the **sun**. But do you think that Pete can **run**?

SCHOOL OF MONSTERS
By Sally Rippin
JAMIE LEE'S BIRTHDAY TREAT
Art by Chris Kennett

Jamie Lee sure likes to **eat**! Today she has a special **treat** ...

When Bat-Boy Tim comes out to **play**, why do others run **away**?

No one likes to be left **out**.
This makes Luna scream and **shout**!

When Will gets nervous, he lets out a **stink**.
But what will all his classmates **think**?

Some monsters are short, and others are **tall**, but Frank is quite clearly the tallest of **all**!

All that Jess touches gets gooey and **sticky**.
How can she solve a problem so **tricky**?

When Bug starts school he cannot **read**.
But Teacher has the help he **needs**!

This is Jem.
She likes to **play**, and thinks up fun new ways each **day**!

Now that you've learned to read along with Sally Rippin's School of Monsters, meet her other friends!

Hey Jack!

Billie B. Brown

Down-to-earth real-life stories for real-life kids!

Billie B. Brown is brave, brilliant and bold, and she always has a creative way to save the day!

Jack has a big heart and an even bigger imagination. He's Billie's best friend, and he'd love to be your friend, too!

Bug's First Day

First American Edition 2023
Kane Miller, A Division of EDC Publishing

Text copyright © 2022 Sally Rippin
Illustration copyright © 2022 Chris Kennett
Series design copyright © 2022 Hardie Grant Children's Publishing
First published in 2022 by Hardie Grant Children's Publishing
Ground Floor, Building 1, 658 Church Street Richmond,
Victoria 3121, Australia.

Kane Miller, A Division of EDC Publishing
5402 S 122nd E Ave, Tulsa, OK 74146
www.kanemiller.com

Library of Congress Control Number: 2022941824

ISBN: 978-1-68464-635-7

Printed in China
by Leo Paper Group
10 9 8 7 6 5 4 3 2 1